Ryan... Jared... and Nathan...

I wish you Summer snowflakes...

winter sparklers... Rainbow circles around the moon!

xoxo

Jim

The Tale
of the Scorpion
and the Caterpillar

The Tale of the Scorpion and the Caterpillar

Written by Jinny Toucan
Illustrated by Terry Stanley

Beaver's Pond Press, Inc.

Edina, Minnesota

Tarik, this one is for you . . .

ISBN 10: 1-59298-267-0
ISBN 13: 978-1-59298-267-7

Library of Congress Control Number: 2008939520
Printed in the United States of America
First Printing: April 2009
13   12   11   10   09   6   5   4   3   2   1

Illustrated by Terry Stanley
Interior design by Clay Schotzko

Beaver's Pond Press, Inc.

Beaver's Pond Press is an imprint of
Beaver's Pond Group
7104 Ohms Lane
Edina, MN 55439-2129
(952) 829-8818
www.BeaversPondPress.com

To order, visit www.BookHouseFulfillment.com
or call 1 (800) 901-3480. Reseller discounts available.

www.scorpionandcaterpillar.com
Email: ginny@jinnytoucan.com

DEDICATION

The Tale of the Scorpion and the Caterpillar is about the loss and transformation that can occur in our lives. On March 27, 2004, my son Tarik became an angel in heaven. Tarik was a wonderful writer and storyteller, and it was through his eyes I was able to write this book. His love of nature and seeing all that is around us each day was an inspiration to me.

As I looked at the lives of scorpions and caterpillars, I realized that loss is as much a part of life as birth. For as we enter this world through birth, we leave a place from which we came, which in a sense is our first loss.

Once I started to think about my loss, I found myself exploring and asking "Why?" I found some answers that proved to be satisfying but some questions remain unanswered.

I hope this book will recapture your childlike openness to explore the possibility that life and love are eternal.

Thank you, Tarik for being my eyes. I dedicate this book to you and your scholarship fund (Tarik Toukan Memorial Scholarship Fund: www.tariktoukan.com).

TRUE FACTS

Queen Butterfly Caterpillar *(Danaus gilippus)* GILI

The Queen caterpillar has bright bands of stripes with drizzles of chocolate browns, yellows, and turquoise. Some have bands of lime-green, black, and yellow. Queen caterpillars feed mainly on two types of milkweed, *Asclepias* and *Sarcostema*. Milkweeds contain glycosides, a toxin that the caterpillar incorporates safely in its body in both the caterpillar and butterfly stages. However, if a bird eats them they are quickly poisoned. They do not die but will temporarily get sick and vomit. The birds learn to avoid eating them. It is very interesting that some species of butterflies have evolved to mimic the color patterns of the Queens and Monarchs. This is called Batesian mimicry.

The Queen butterfly is a large chocolate brown butterfly. Its wings have a few white spots and are edged with black. The Monarch butterfly has black veins on the top of its body and is generally a lighter color with flecks of orange, and is larger than the Queen butterfly.

Butterflies go through a cycle of life called "complete metamorphosis." The cycle starts with an egg. The egg hatches into a caterpillar. The caterpillar eats, grows, and sheds its tough skin several times as it grows. The caterpillar then transforms into a pupa or chrysalis (which looks like a lime-green cocoon that hangs like a jack-o-lantern with trim of gold dots). Out of this cocoon the adult butterfly emerges. The adult butterfly sips nectar, mates, and lays eggs. The cycle is complete.

Superstition Mountain Scorpion *(Superstitioniidae)* **DAEV**

Superstitioniidae are interesting scorpions that include five genera and ten species. Most of these scorpions are troglobites (cave dwellers) and can be found in wet caves in subtropical parts of Mexico and South America. These scorpions lack eyes and pigmentation. They range in color from black to pale yellow (two tribes: *Superstitionini*—darker—and *Typhlochactini*—pale). They are quite large (around 70 mm long).

One of the most interesting things about scorpions is that they fluoresce under ultraviolet light, due to complex substances in the epidermis that makes it impermeable. Scorpions are nocturnal (active at night) arachnids (class of insect *Arachnida*, also including spiders, mites, and ticks). No data has been found about the venom of these scorpions, and they are probably harmless.

CHAPTER 1

Gili and Daev

Scorpions don't bite; they sting with quick whips of their tails.

Deep in the Sonoran Desert in Mexico lived a Queen butterfly caterpillar (official name: *Danaus giliippus*) named Gili. She was not only the princess of her small kingdom, but also the most beautiful of all the other caterpillars. Her body was a mass of fine turquoise and gold stripes with hints of chocolate drizzled throughout. As delicious as she looked, the birds avoided her because she ate milkweeds, which contain chemicals that are safe for caterpillars but poisonous to birds. This was good for Gili because the birds were reluctant to harm her when she basked in the sun and feasted on her favorite milkweed plants. Life was easy, yet Gili was lonely and felt that there must be more to life than eating lovely milkweed plants. She was young and felt there was a big world out there, and she wanted to learn more about it.

In the same desert lived a light-gold scorpion (official name: *Superstitioniidae*) named Daev. He was young, strong, and rather large for a scorpion. His body was covered with fine hairs with which he could feel the vibrations made by prey and by any creature that might come close enough to harm him. Like many of his species, Daev was born without eyes and had no pigmentation. As a result, he had to be very careful of the sun. As frightening as it looked, the stinger at the end of his tail contained no poison. But Daev was not aware that his tail had no venom, and neither were his prey. So he thought he would be a match for any predator. Though Daev was very proud and fearless, deep inside he had a tender heart. But he had an image to keep up. Not only was he heir to the scorpion throne, but he was also the largest, strongest, and most courageous scorpion of them all. Yet he, like Gili, felt that his life was missing something. He felt that the other scorpions did not really know him, and that there was more to life than just being aggressive.

CHAPTER 2
Metal Monsters

"A caterpillar who seeks to know herself would
never become a butterfly." —Andre Gide

There were a lot of changes happening in this desert. Giant metal monsters were chewing up the land. Daev could feel the vibrations of their movements and knew they did not belong there: they were intruders. They made clanking noises and such heavy vibrations that he knew they were larger than he was, so they must be monsters. Daev would follow the vibrations to find out. How dare they challenge his supremacy! He sucked in his stomach and marched off to fight this terrible foe.

Meanwhile, Gili was restless on her milkweed, so she decided to explore more of her world. Her kingdom had been suffering from a plague that took the lives of the elderly. Maybe she could find a cure out there in the desert. She, too, set off in search of answers. As she walked, she felt the earth vibrate beneath her feet and in the distance she saw a huge creature she had never seen before, one with a body that glistened in the sun. She decided to get a closer look and followed the vibrations. The intruder seemed to get bigger the closer she got, though it was still far away. It was monsterous!

The journey to get close to the monsters took weeks for both Gili and Daev. Gili had feasted on her favorite milkweed before leaving and had a full stomach. She enjoyed sunning herself during the day and resting in the evening on any bush or flower along the way. Daev traveled by night, as the sun was his enemy. Sometimes, when it got too hot, he burrowed into the ground or retreated into the rocks nearby.

After weeks of traveling, both Daev and Gili could sense how big the monster was compared to them. "Things always look smaller when you view them from a distance," thought Gili. Even though Daev could not see, his senses told him that this monster was huge. The desert looked amazing as it spread across the horizon like a beige velvet carpet. Because there were no trees and few bushes, it was easy to spot any intruders. As both Gili and Daev walked across the desert, the sunbeams shown upon the metal monsters and made their armor glisten like jewels.

The monsters were busy chewing up the soil and tossing piles of dirt into tidy mounds. Close up to the monster, Gili and Daev felt an overpowering fear. Daev then knew that this monster was much too big for him to fight, so he decided to retreat to his kingdom. Gili also decided that she really didn't need to know any more about this monster: life was just fine back home. As Gili turned and began to hurry back home, she caught a glimpse of Daev. She had never seen a scorpion before, and he reminded her of the metal monster. She was bored of all the caterpillars in her kingdom and Daev was different: his golden body sparkled in the sun. "How exciting!" she thought. "Someone my size, and so handsome, strong, and so different from me!"

Daev, too, was leaving and although he could not see Gili and her beautiful stripes, he could feel her vibrations. He stopped to as-

4

sess the situation. Was she an enemy, like the metal monster, ready to pounce on him? Gili stopped too, as she could see his fear, but she enjoyed the excitement that rippled through her body. Surprisingly, Gili found Daev intriguing and not as ominous as he looked.

All of a sudden one of the metal monsters quickly moved its pincers down, down, down, as it chewed up the very earth they were standing on. They heard a loud *CRUNCH* as the earth gave way, and they were tossed into the air. Dirt encased them as if they

were buried underground in a tomb. When they landed, they found themselves on top of each other, and fear once again enveloped them in a cocoon as they clung to each other for safety. They were encased in dirt, but Daev curled around Gili, his armor surrounding her like a protective shield. Gili cried in fear and whimpered, "I'm so frightened. Are we going to die?" Daev held Gili closer and said, "Don't worry I will keep you safe."

It had all happened so quickly that Daev hadn't had much time to think about anything but surviving this frightening experience. Gili was safe, protected by his golden armor. Daev could feel Gili trembling so he gently said "Life has a way of throwing us into situations we can't control." Gili smiled and feeling somewhat better, replied, "Yes, our reactions can sometimes surprise us."

CHAPTER 3

Seeking Shelter

Scorpions have existed in some form for about 425–450 million years.

They found themselves dumped in a pile. The world was silent. Daev could sense the vibrations above and knew he had to get Gili to climb upward and out of the mass of earth. Before long, they broke through the dirt and into the sunlight, and quickly assessed where they were. All around them were piles of soil. The metal monster was busy chewing up yet another spot farther away. With Gili on his back, Daev made his way down the mound and started heading for some rocks that were piled up against a small mountain. It took them most of the day and part of the evening to arrive at their destination. Gili was in shock and had injured her foot. Daev was still feeling strong and in excellent shape.

Once within the shelter of the rocks, Gili noticed that Daev glowed in the moonlight. He looked so handsome, his armor shimmering like a star in the night sky. At that instant, he became her hero, her knight in shining armor. Daev felt Gili's foot and quickly made a paste of dirt mixed with water from a nearby broken leaf and spread it on her injured foot. Gili felt instant relief from the pain. "Th…thank you so much for saving me from the monster," she stammered. Daev was speechless and lay down in the cool dirt. Although Gili feared that the metal monster would return, she was so exhausted that she sank into a deep and restful sleep. Before closing her eyes though, she noticed that Daev had moved to the entrance of their rock cave to stand guard. Wanting to keep them both safe, he had taken the position so that he would be sure to feel any vibrations that were unnatural for the quiet evening.

When the sun rose in the morning, Gili woke up and headed for the opening in the rocks. The sun soothed her tired body, and her foot seemed already healed. Daev was startled by her movement, and he sprang to his feet, his tail lashing out in fear.

Gili quickly introduced herself. "I'm Gili," she said. "Don't worry. I think we're safe. What's your name?"

Daev, embarrassed by his reaction, quietly answered, "Daev." He slowly sighed with relief and went back to his spot on the ground. Gili then realized that Daev was blind and reacted only to movements and vibrations.

Gili told Daev about her home and the milkweed bushes that she dined on and that one day she would be queen of her kingdom. She also told him about her lovely turquoise and gold stripes and how her family wanted her to marry someone from the royal family. She hadn't known that other species existed in her small kingdom.

Daev was silent at first, but then he started to talk about his life. He was also royalty, yet had always felt that he didn't fit into his society. He had assumed that everyone was a blind scorpion like he was. "We survived a most terrifying adventure, and when I held you close to me you were so soft and furry. I liked that. Although I couldn't see you, Gili, I knew you were beautiful and different from anyone or anything I've ever known," Daev said shyly. He instinctively wanted to protect her and keep her safe from harm. Daev was still not sure who or what Gili was—she couldn't be a scorpion, since scorpions eat ants and other insects, not milkweed bushes, and they are not soft and furry—but he knew that he wanted to be her friend. Gili smiled and said, "Daev, I am so happy that life put us together, and in you, I've found a new friend."

CHAPTER 4
The Return Home

Butterflies sip liquid using a proboscis, a tube-like tongue.

They quickly became friends and set off on the long, perilous journey home. Gili was comforted knowing that Daev was with her, and Daev was happy to be in her company.

Gili suggested that they leave quickly because she could see the metal monsters in the distance devouring more and more of the earth. She was frightened that they would eventually come to their very spot. But Daev preferred to travel by night as his senses were much keener in the coolness of the night air. However, Gili, accustomed to seeing her way in the sunlight, felt ill at ease traveling by night. While they were discussing their travel plans, Daev felt a tremble in the earth that sent him scurrying in a circle. Yes, Gili was right. It would be best to leave quickly. Gili would ride on his back and protect him from the harsh sunlight, and they would keep close to the rocks and other vegetation on their way home. This way, Daev would be sheltered from the sun if it got too hot.

The sun beat down on them as they traveled, and Gili enjoyed its warmth on her body. Daev felt large and very strong as he marched through the desert like a soldier, his florescent armor reflecting the sun's light. They walked for hours, with Daev seeking occasional shelter from the sun.

They continued throughout the day and eventually decided to rest while the sun was setting. Gili was hungry and missed her daily meals of milkweed, and Daev was too exhausted to think of food. It was hard work carrying Gili on his back, and he was not accustomed to the extreme temperatures. Gili went in search of food and water among the rocks while Daev slept, catching up on some much-needed sleep. As Gili searched among the rocks, she saw a milkweed bush not too far away. She was so excited that she forgot to keep a lookout for danger. And just then, a desert mouse popped out of a hole—with its mouth open!

When the mouse lunged, Gili was so startled that she fell off the rock; the mouse missed! Daev felt the vibrations of her fall and raced to her side. The mouse was about to make a second attempt, but Daev blocked it with his pincers, his tail lashing and striking at the mouse until he hit it on the nose. Although Daev's stinger did not contain poison, its sharp point could still penetrate the mouse's

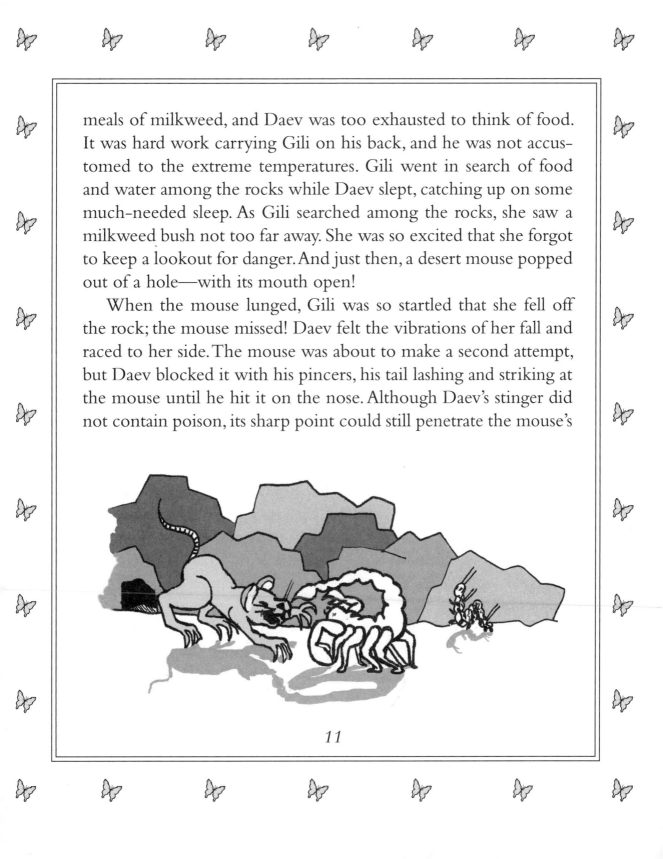

sensitive skin. The mouse shrieked in pain and scurried back into its hole. Once again, Gili was grateful to have such a wonderful friend as Daev, so she hobbled over to him and gave him a kiss on his head. Daev had never been kissed by anyone but his mother before, and he ran back to the rocks in complete embarrassment. Gili saw Daev was shy, but she also thought that he was so brave to face such perils.

Gili continued on to her milkweed bush and ate her full. She was also able to find a little water caught on an upturned leaf, which she carefully dragged back to Daev. He was happy to drink the cool liquid, but he was starting to get hungry. He told Gili to stay in the rocks while he went to find food for himself. Soon, Daev was dining on ants and other small insects he found in the rocks. He returned with his stomach full, and they both went to sleep.

Very early in the morning, while it was still dark, Daev decided to continue their journey home. Gili understood that he preferred to travel by night because of the harsh sun, so they set off together. He didn't need to carry Gili now because her foot was healed.

They traveled for nearly a week, sometimes by day, and sometimes by night, stopping to rest along the way and eat their fill of milkweed and insects. They were a strange pair indeed—a scorpion and a caterpillar.

One night when Daev was out looking for food, an owl spied him. Of course, Daev's warning system depended on vibrations from the ground and did not detect the approaching bird. But Gili saw it! Knowing that most birds avoided her because she was poisonous to them, Gili quickly jumped on Daev's back. The owl screeched in horror and flew up into the sky. Daev was astonished by Gili's bravery, and somehow he felt embarrassed, so he quickly retreated into the rocks. Gili knew how proud he was, and she did not need a "thank you" for saving his life. They had been having long talks during the day and night, and he had told her that his upbringing required him to be brave, armored, afraid of nothing, and able to defend himself at all times. Deep inside, though, Daev was loving and sensitive, although he didn't know how to show it, and he didn't tell this to Gili.

Gili went about settling down for the night and did not bring up the incident with the owl again. It was enough for her to know that Daev loved her. She could see it in his kindness and how gently he treated her.

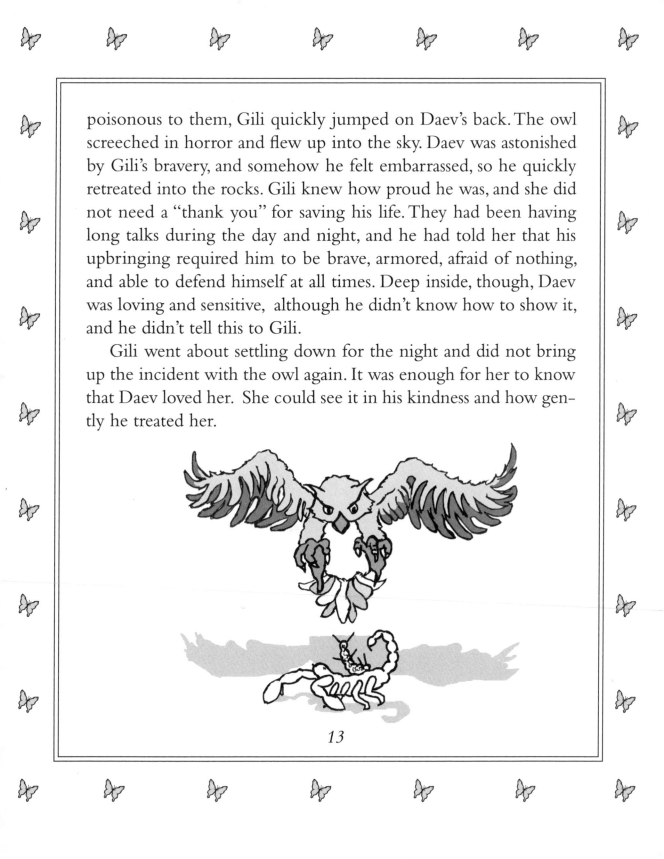

13

CHAPTER 5

A Strange Pair

*It is a myth that scorpions sting themselves
to death when surrounded by fire.*

After a few weeks, and many near-death experiences with predators, Daev and Gili made it back to their homes. The moment
came when they needed to go their separate ways. They stood at
the crossroads that divided their kingdoms, Gili holding back her
tears because she did not want to leave Daev. Daev stood stiffly in
his armor and awkwardly grunted, "Good-bye." Then he turned,
walked away, and did not look back. Gili stood at the crossroads
weeping because she was saying good-bye to a dear friend. Then
all of a sudden, Daev stopped, turned, and ran back toward Gili. He
wrapped his arms around her and told her that he loved her.

This time Daev did all the talking, and he told her that he could
not live without her. They had shared so many long talks during their journey. Gili had learned what a scorpion was, and Daev
somehow came to understand what kind of creature Gili was. Now
they knew that they couldn't be apart. But they both knew how
unusual the other was, and that neither of their societies would
understand how they could be friends, let alone love each other.
What were they to do? How could they explain everything to their
families?

Daev insisted that Gili come home with him. "After all," he
exclaimed, "my species of scorpion cannot see. Perhaps they would

think you are just like them. Please, Gili, come back to my kingdom and meet my parents."

Gili was overjoyed because she loved Daev and did not want to continue her life without him. "Oh, yes, Daev! I would love to, and just think, it will be another adventure," laughed Gili. So they made their way to Daev's kingdom.

CHAPTER 6

Daev's Kingdom

It is a myth that a butterfly flying in one's face is a
sign of immediate cold weather to come.

Daev's kingdom was inside a dark, damp cave. Upon entering the cave, Gili saw a host of scorpions, all glowing like the lights in the distant hills of the desert and twinkling in their dark crevices. Some of them crawled slowly across the ceiling, reminding Gili of stars moving across the sky. It was such a magical and beautiful place, so different from Gili's kingdom of milkweed and desert flowers. Although Gili and Dave were both desert dwellers, their lives were different. Gili was so excited that she could hardly wait to meet Daev's family and friends.

Daev was much larger than all the other scorpions, and Gili could immediately see how much respect and love they had for him. All the scorpions in his kingdom surrounded him, chanting his name and hailing him for his bravery in facing the intruding monsters. Gili felt almost invisible, and in a way she was, because none of the scorpions had eyes. Nevertheless, she felt they could sense her presence. She was so much smaller than most of the scorpions, but this did not frighten her. She knew deep in her heart that Daev was her loving friend. He would never let anything bad happen to her.

Suddenly, the great crowd of scorpions parted and two scorpions, Daev's mother and father, appeared. His father was much smaller than Daev, but very fit. And despite his size, when he spoke his voice boomed out, "Daev, did you slay the monsters?"

Daev told him that the monster was metal and was the size of seven hundred caves all piled on top of each other! It would take a giant scorpion to slay such a monster! Daev's father hung his head in disappointment and said, "I hope you tried your best." Daev's mother pushed by her husband and gave her son a big hug. "At least you were brave enough to face such a giant," she said.

Everyone cheered and applauded Daev. Daev's mother was petite and graceful, and there was kindness in her smile and tender-

ness in her touch. Then she said, "Daev, aren't you going to introduce us to your friend?" Daev quickly put his arm around Gili and said, "This is Gili. We met along the way. She was also planning to slay the metal monster." Gili was speechless, as that had not been her intention at all! But she wasn't going to argue, and she nodded, hoping Daev's parents could feel the vibrations.

Turning in Gili's direction, Daev's father asked, "Do you speak?"

"Y-y-yes, I d-d-do," Gili faltered.

"Well then, tell us your story," Daev's father said.

But Daev interrupted. "Father, we've been traveling for weeks and we're exhausted. We just want to rest and get some food."

CHAPTER 7

The Scorpion Banquet

Because we focused on the snake we missed the scorpion.
—Egyptian proverb

The kingdom was buzzing. A banquet was to be served in honor of Daev and his brave and perilous journey to slay the metal monster.

Before the feast, Daev showed Gili his room. Gili was delighted to see a small crevice in the rock through which shone the moonlight and starlight. She was delighted because she didn't think she could live without seeing the sun or stars again. But Daev said that the crack only let in a little bit of light, and that the room was not very bright during the day. Of course, he only knew this by feeling the sunlight. It didn't matter to Gili; she was with her precious Daev, the scorpion who was strong and fearless yet so tender that it made her heart melt.

As they stood talking about his room, Daev's mother came to the door to inform them that their seats at the banquet were ready. Everyone was waiting for Daev's entrance. Daev was very nervous because only he knew that Gili was a caterpillar; he did not want anyone to get too close to her and find out that she was different. He told Gili not to tell them who she was, and to pretend to eat the food they served.

"Daev, what do they serve?" she asked innocently.

"Oh, mostly insects, small lizards—our great delicacy—and a few centipedes."

"What?" Gili exclaimed in horror. "My mother once told me that we had an uncle who was part centipede!"

Daev quickly corrected himself. "Oh, I'm sorry, Gili. I meant to say centipede mice."

"What's a centipede mouse?" Gili asked.

"Um, it is a rare mouse found around the rocks near this kingdom," he replied.

"Ugh!" Gili said. She found this all disgusting because she only ate plants!

It was getting late, so they quickly ended their conversation and rushed to the banquet. "Gili," Daev whispered as they went down the hall, "don't forget: let me do most of the talking."

As Daev and Gili entered the banquet room, everyone stood up. Daev strode by with Gili tucked neatly underneath his large muscular frame. Daev told the servants that he did not want anyone seated next to him or his guest. Everyone honored his wishes, and the attendants quickly reseated several guests.

The feast began and Gili was amazed at how much food was on the table. She graciously accepted everything they put on her plate, but because she found it disgusting and no one could see, Gili quietly pushed the plate away from her. However, there was plenty of water and Gili drank her fill. Daev loaded his plate repeatedly. She hadn't known that he could eat so much. The cave was filled with crunching and munching. At one point Gili actually thought she saw part of a centipede, but she wasn't certain because it was so dark. Everything was so strange—so different from her world among the milkweed bushes—yet fascinating.

After the feast, several scorpions gave very boring speeches but heaped a lot of praise on Daev and his family. After the feast but before going to bed, Gili quietly asked Daev if there was anything she could eat. Daev had totally forgotten about Gili. He was so exhausted from the trip. But he slipped out of the cave in search of milkweed bushes. It was night, his favorite time. To Gili, it seemed like hours before he returned, carrying bunches and bunches of delicious milkweed. Gili squealed in delight, and then ate until she fell into a deep and rest- ful sleep, her first peaceful rest in weeks.

CHAPTER 8
Fighting Scorpions

"The butterfly counts not months but moments, and has time enough."
—*Rabindranath Tagore*

In the morning, the sun shone very dimly through the crevice, just as Daev had predicted. Gili was so excited to see the sun that she jumped up and crawled out of the crevice. It was delightful, and she sat sunning herself and enjoying the warmth on her body. Daev slept most of the day, as did the entire kingdom. While they slept, Gili crawled down from the cave and went searching for milkweed. "It is such a glorious day," she thought. Then she saw a huge scorpion heading her way, his pincers clicking together and his tail lashing the air. Gili could see a grimace on his mouth. He looked just as the scorpions had looked when they were eating at the feast.

"Help!" cried Gili, crawling away as fast as she could. The beast cornered her between some rocks, and she closed her eyes, waiting for the worst.

Suddenly the scorpion flipped up in the air. Daev was upon him. "How dare you treat my guest in such a manner?" screamed Daev. "You are banished from our kingdom!" Humiliated, the other scorpion scurried away, his tail dragging behind him.

Daev quickly brought Gili back to the cave. To her great surprise, he shouted at her. "Don't ever get into another situation like this again, Gili!"

Gili was horrified at the way he was speaking to her. This was a side of Daev that she hadn't known. She felt he would have killed the other scorpion, and this frightened her. Daev instructed Gili to stay inside the cave and *never* go out again without asking his permission.

Daev stormed out of the door, leaving Gili in the dark room weeping her heart out. "What has happened to Daev?" she asked herself. "Why has he changed?" Gili didn't know that Daev was trying to live up to his tough image and he didn't want his tenderness to be confused with weakness.

CHAPTER 9
The Moment of Truth

Scorpions can survive high levels or radiation.

Days and weeks passed, and each day, Daev became more nervous and angry. Gili hardly went out into the sunshine, and she became sick and depressed. Even though Daev brought her fresh milkweed daily, she was listless and quiet.

One day when Daev was out hunting, his mother paid Gili a visit. Daev's mother was gentle and loving. She reminded Gili of the way Daev was during their journey back from the metal monster. "Tell me about yourself, Gili," she said. "Do you live around here?"

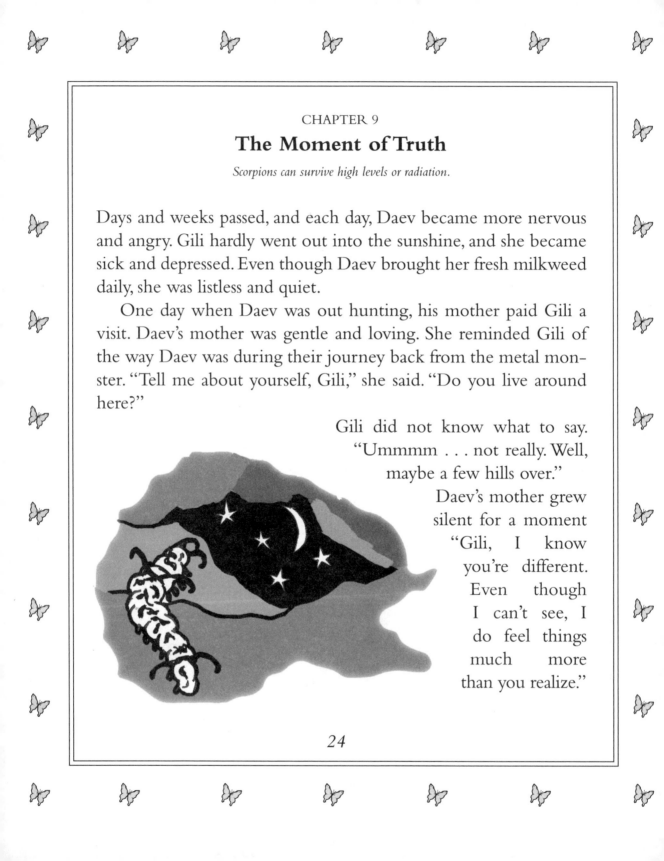

Gili did not know what to say. "Ummmm . . . not really. Well, maybe a few hills over."

Daev's mother grew silent for a moment "Gili, I know you're different. Even though I can't see, I do feel things much more than you realize."

Gili started to weep and she told Daev's mother the truth about who she was, and how she had met Daev. It felt so good to be honest and get it all off her chest.

Daev's mother admired Gili's bravery for telling the truth. She said, "Sometimes bravery takes a different face, a more powerful one, when it comes to telling the truth. We don't have to slay monsters to prove our strength or worth. The biggest strength is in our souls and hearts. Telling the truth is the bravest act of all! Cowards hide behind their lies, but the brave tell the truth."

Daev's mother immediately fell in love with Gili, and knew her son had her soft and gentle nature, and kind heart. "Don't worry, I am always here for you, and Daev loves you very much, I know. However, my husband does not share my feelings, so please be careful with your words. The truth is between us now, and the kingdom must know it very soon. But Daev must be the one to tell everyone. This will prove to me, and to all of us, that Daev is as strong as I think he is, both inside and out."

After Daev's mother had gone, Gili cried. "She is so wonderful," Gili thought. "I know where Daev gets his tenderness."

Daev returned home a few hours later in a bad mood. When Gili told Daev that his mother had come to visit, Daev went into a rage. He lashed his tail, striking Gili so hard she flipped across the room. She was shocked. He had never struck her before. Gili began to cry, but she was angry, too! She screamed at Daev. "All you do is creep around all day ready to pounce and use your stinger on some defenseless creature. Then you return home to control me and block me from living my own life. You make my life miserable because you are miserable yourself. You are an angry, ugly creature, dragging your venomous tail. You may walk backward at times, but you never learn where you've been. Your brute force is not bravery. Telling the truth: that takes much more bravery! I'm not afraid of you, and you cannot do this to me. I will not allow it!"

Then Gili broke down and sobbed uncontrollably. Daev was so ashamed of what he had done that he retreated, dragging his tail behind him. Gili then realized how much she missed her home, the sunshine, and the delicious milkweed leaves that tasted so much better when she ate them off the bush, not dragged for hours in the sand until all the moisture was dried out of them. She brushed herself off and started toward the door when Daev returned, blocking her exit.

"Where are you going?" he demanded.

"I'm going home, Daev," Gili announced. "I cannot live in the dark, telling lies, and eating dried-out milkweed. For once in your life, stand up and tell the truth, Daev. Or are you too frightened?"

Daev paced the room, his tail lashing out uncontrollably. He then announced that he was going to make a decision. He called for an immediate meeting of the entire kingdom.

CHAPTER 10
Daev's Speech

Females lay eggs on the underside of milkweed leaves.

Within minutes everyone in the kingdom was assembled to hear what Daev wanted to say. Daev's father worried that it had something to do with Gili, and Daev's mother was so happy for her son, for she could feel his love for Gili. Daev had been lonely for quite some time and constantly pretended to be fierce. His mother knew that Daev was kind and gentle inside.

Daev stood on the stone that served as a podium, announcing that he was in love with a caterpillar. He also told his shocked subjects that he wanted to go to her kingdom to meet her family. He would be back, but needed to have a different perspective on other creatures. He felt that this would help him rule his own kingdom more fairly and have a wider vision of the future. Daev was a superb speaker and everyone listened. Soon he had them eating out of his pincers. Daev's father listened with his mouth hanging open, but his mother couldn't have been prouder.

After saying farewell to his family, Daev and Gili began their journey to her family on the other side of the hill. Gili could see the greenery in the distance, but it was too far to see anything distinctly; it was at least a four-day walk. They were quiet while they walked. Gili was still angry at him, but Daev's thoughts were of his speech and how excited he felt about experiencing a new place. Daev loved adventure.

CHAPTER 11

A Loss of Confidence

Young scorpions are born one by one and are carried on their mothers' back
until able to survive on their own.

After walking most of the day, they took refuge between some rocks for the evening. Gili had calmed down and said, "Daev, I'm worried about your temper."

Daev explained that he was under a lot of pressure from his family and because of his position in the kingdom. "I'm sorry, Gili, that I lost control of my tail and flipped you over," Daev said in embarrassment.

They both ended up laughing at what had happened and soon fell asleep after such a long and a tiring day.

The next morning, they pressed on. During the day, Gili rode on Daev's back to protect him from the sun, and sometimes they walked through the night. As they came nearer to Gili's kingdom, Daev started to lose his confidence. "You called me an angry, ugly creature, Gili. Did you mean that?" Gili cuddled up to Daev's chest and whispered, "I love you. I only said that because when you get angry you look ugly."

They both laughed, but Gili could see that Daev was losing his confidence. So she told him a bit about her family and what he should expect. "Everyone in my family is very colorful. My mother is turquoise and pink, and my father is turquoise and gold with bits of violet. I guess I take after my dad. Of course, you won't be able to see them, but maybe you can imagine what they are like."

"Remember how you held me the first time we met?" she went on. "You told me how furry and soft I felt. That's what my whole family is like. Everyone seems like me on the outside, but I can assure you that no one thinks like I do. Everyone else is happy living in the sunshine and eating milkweed, but for some reason I felt that I needed more. I was also determined to find a cure for the plague that threatens our community, though I guess I didn't do that. Inside I'm different, just like you're different from your subjects."

Gili paused, then said thoughtfully, "Fate somehow brought us together in the pincers of the metal monster. I have certainly learned a lot more than the other caterpillars in my kingdom. It's been a fun adventure, don't you think, Daev?"

They both chuckled. What a strange sight, a scorpion and a caterpillar. "But the difference between your kingdom and mine," continued Gili, "is that caterpillars can see. They will immediately see that you are different than us. Some may recognize that you are a scorpion. There are no lies in my kingdom. So don't be surprised if you don't get a warm welcome. And I'm sure that many will know that scorpions eat centipedes. But they won't see who you are inside. In that way, your kingdom is superior to ours."

She saw that Daev seemed worried, so Gili reassuringly said, "I will ride on your back when we enter the kingdom so that everyone will know you will not harm them."

Daev felt embarrassed again, and a little frightened, too. "What if no one likes me?" he thought. Everyone in his own kingdom bowed down to him. How would he handle rejection?

CHAPTER 12

Gili's Kingdom

*Monarch caterpillars eat poisonous milkweed leaves so that toxins will be
in their bodies, making them poisonous to predators.*

As luck would have it, Daev and Gili arrived in the caterpillar kingdom during the night. Almost everyone was sleeping, so full of milkweed they could hardly move. Gili quickly brought Daev to her personal quarters in the royal palace, and they went to sleep immediately. It had been a long, tough journey home, with many predators trying to eat them, and they were emotionally and physically exhausted.

The next morning the sun shone through the leaves that encased their room. Although Daev could not see, he could sense the brightness and could smell the lush greenery. Gili took him to the shadiest corner of the room so he could rest without the sun bothering him. He was comfortable in the damp shade, and he loved the peacefulness of his corner.

Gili told him to go back to sleep; she knew that most scorpions sleep during the day. Then she went outside to find her family. Rows of flowers graced the pathway to her parents' quarters. Upon reaching their part of the palace, she was stopped by the guards. They were delighted to see Princess Gili back after her long journey, but they had some distressing news. Both her parents had fallen victim to the plague, a disease from which all caterpillars eventually suffer. Royal servants had found her parents wrapped and bound in lime green slime. The casing had eventually dried up, and soon after they were never seen again.

When she heard the news, Gili could not stop sobbing. The thought of losing her parents broke her heart. She loved them so much, and she knew they would have loved Daev, despite his size and species. Now the kingdom awaited their Queen Gili. It was time to rejoice in her return. But Gili was in no mood to celebrate after discovering the sad news of her loving parents. Overcome in deep sadness, she returned to her room and sobbed. When Daev learned what had happened, he put his pincers around her to comfort her.

Gili explained to Daev that her little kingdom suffered from a plague that killed the older generation and at times young adults, too. "Daev, this is something we live with and one of the reasons I left my kingdom was to go in search of a cure for this most dreaded disease," said Gili.

"Oh, Gili, if there is anything I can do to help, please know I am here for you," replied Daev.

"Daev, please stay in my room until I finish my speech and after I am crowned the new queen. I will then inform everyone that I am in love with you. They will meet you later in the evening during the banquet."

CHAPTER 13
Gili's Coronation Speech

It is a myth that all scorpions are poisonous.

Everyone in the kingdom turned out for the coronation of Queen Gili. She looked beautiful with the sun glistening off of her turquoise and gold body. By now, the hints of chocolate swirls on her body were fading and she looked like a sparkling diamond. Everyone was delighted to see her back.

Gili began her speech:

"My fellow caterpillars. I am so deeply touched by all the love and support you have given me upon my return. With a heavy heart, I will officially announce the recent passing of my parents, King Lippus and Queen Dana. They loved this kingdom and were so proud of everyone and also of the milkweed that grows here. I hope I can live up to my parent's expectations and the expectations of everyone here in the kingdom. I will serve you the best way I can, and continue to rule with love, just like my parents did."

Everyone cheered and some caterpillars in the crowd were moved to tears when one of the palace subjects placed a flowered crown on Gili's head during the coronation ceremony. Queen Gili was much loved.

As he waited in Gili's chamber, Daev listened to her beautiful speech. He was so proud of Gili and loved her more than ever, if that was possible.

Gili then told the crowd that she had an unusual guest with her who she would bring to the banquet that evening. She expected everyone to be on their best behavior because the guest was heir to the throne of his own kingdom and would soon be a king. The little caterpillar kingdom was buzzing with speculation about who this guest could be.

Gili returned to her chamber and collapsed into bed. She was exhausted and did not feel well. Daev was worried about making a good impression during the banquet, but when he went to speak to Gili about it, he found her sound asleep.

CHAPTER 14

The Caterpillar Banquet

It is a myth that butterflies are good luck.

As the evening came, Daev, being nocturnal, became more alert and woke Gili up. She quickly got herself ready for the banquet. She explained to Daev that caterpillars didn't usually dine at night, but because he was their guest, she thought it would be polite to have their banquet in the evening.

Gili climbed onto Daev's back as they made their entrance into the main dining hall in the center of the kingdom. It was fortunate that Daev was blind, because Gili could see the look of terror on every caterpillar's face. Some of the older ones fainted, and others crawled away in fear. Others stood there in shock, their multiple feet glued to the ground. Daev could sense the fear in the caterpillars, which made him feel awkward and out of place.

No one had the courage to sit close to Daev. The entire head table remained empty except for Daev and Queen Gili.

The servants bowed to Queen Gili and quickly placed fresh milkweed and nectar on the table. Daev could not understand why anyone would want to eat milkweed and drink nectar. Of course, water was served and Daev drank some. Only Gili could see the fear in the other caterpillars, but Daev continued to sense it and this made him feel sad and unwanted.

At the end of the banquet Queen Gili made a short speech. She decided to tell the truth and admitted to everyone that she had left the kingdom in search of a cure for the plague and also because she had felt that there were many things to learn about life outside of their kingdom. She told them that during her perilous trip she was rescued by Daev on numerous occasions.

"Even though he is not like us," she continued, "we should not pass judgment on who he is inside his shell. Fate put us together, in the pincers of the metal monster, and Daev protected me from boulders and the weight of the earth, all of which could have crushed me. For this I am deeply indebted to him, and as my fellow caterpillars, you should honor him for his bravery and thank him for saving my life."

She paused, looking around the room. "His life is totally unlike ours. He does not eat milkweed and is sensitive to the sun. But we should not condemn him for being different from us. He has a kingdom much like ours, and loving parents, too. It's true that he eats some things that we would not, but give him a chance to prove himself. If you can only look inside his hard golden armor, you will find he has a loving and sensitive heart."

The crowd was won over by Gili's moving speech. Everyone clapped and whistled and started chanting

Daev's name. They loved him because he had saved their queen. But most of all, they cheered the fact that Gili was brave enough to tell the truth, to take a risk, and to share her innermost feelings with all of them. This made her the bravest one of all.

If Daev had possessed eyes, he would have had tears in them. Then the strangest thing happened. He felt a little moisture just above his mouth where his eyes would have been: not a tear, just moisture. Gili noticed this, too, but never said a word. Daev was a very special scorpion, and they were such a strange pair—a scorpion and a caterpillar.

Daev felt strange, too. Despite being blind, he could almost visualize what Gili looked like, her soft, furry body the colors she described. Although he had never seen any colors with his eyes, he could somehow see them in his mind. He didn't say anything, but he wondered. Was it his soul that made him see? He didn't know. "Some things cannot be explained," he thought. But he knew he felt different. "We can't see air, but it moves the trees. We can't see our thoughts, but we dream and see things in our minds," he thought. Daev could not explain what was happening.

In the weeks that followed, Daev enjoyed his stay with the caterpillars. At first he could sense their fear, but eventually they grew accustomed to him, and he was helpful lifting heavy objects for them and fighting off predators. In return, they protected Daev from owls by jumping on his back to camouflage him.

CHAPTER 15
Daev's Journey Home

Scorpions have chelicerae, claw-like structures that protrude
from their mouths enabling them to chew.

Soon, however, Daev longed to see his family again, even though everyone was so nice to him. Gili did not want him to leave, but she fully understood that he needed to see his family and subjects. He promised her that he would return in exactly two weeks because he could not stand to be away from her for longer than that. She laughed and he hugged her with his pincers and she kissed him. Daev was embarrassed and left at once. She called out to him to be careful and to keep close to the rocks.

Gili kept herself busy while Daev was gone, but she noticed that she lacked energy, and that the stripes were fading from her body. Everyone told her that it was because she missed Daev so much. She dreamed of faraway places and of traveling with Daev, and she kept wondering where her parents had really gone. Were they now in some other world? Was it like her own world, or was it different? Although her kingdom kept her busy, she was not herself. But all of her subjects continued to rejoice about her return to them because she was so kind and gentle.

Daev had a wonderful visit with his family. His mother was especially happy to see him. The kingdom held a feast for him, and everyone rejoiced all night. "Daev, you have chosen wisely and I love Gili very much," said Daev's mother. "All I ever wanted was for you to be happy, and you are."

Later that night Daev's father made a suggestion. "Maybe you should meet one of the young scorpions I personally selected to be your bride. Many are fine specimens, I might add," his father proudly said. Daev lost his temper and shouted, "I can make my own decisions, thank you, and I will be soon returning to Gili. Don't worry, I will visit you and Mom now and then. We are only a four-day walk from here." Daev's father, although not completely satisfied, retreated. Daev was his only offspring, and he did not want to upset him.

Daev was always such an eloquent speaker, and both parents always seemed to give in after listening to his reasoning. So at midnight, Daev headed back to the valley. Ten days had passed and he had promised Gili that he would be back within two weeks.

CHAPTER 16
Return to Queen Gili

Scorpions run from danger or remain still, and they are timid.
Their sting is similar to a bee sting.

His journey back was treacherous, since it was the season of the owls. Several times they swooped down to attack him. Somehow he managed to escape them. Living with the caterpillars, he had learned how to camouflage himself with leaves, and he could now sense the shadows of birds passing overhead. Perhaps this was his imagination, but perhaps there was more to it. Like Gili, he wondered if there was more to everything than what he could sense.

Daev returned to the kingdom of the caterpillars early in the morning. He found the mood in this normally busy kingdom quiet and solemn. Everyone knew Daev, but it seemed to him that they greeted him reluctantly, and he could sense a feeling of sadness. When he arrived at the palace, the guards quickly took him aside and told him the most distressing news. Gili had fallen ill with the plague and had then disappeared. Daev reacted angrily. Screaming with grief, he lashed his tail at the guards who had brought the news. He tore the room apart, then collapsed on the floor in misery. And for the first time in his life, real tears welled up in the little hole above his mouth. He was confused by them, but they kept coming. His body shook with sobs. He was devastated.

When Daev recovered enough to be aware of his surroundings, he sensed something hanging in the corner of the room. Reaching out, his pincers felt a strange, dry sack. He remembered that Gili had once described this to him. It was dry and felt as if it would crumble to pieces. In his anger, he ripped it down and tore it into shreds. This was the thing that had taken his dear Gili away from him! He wanted to destroy it completely. But the sack didn't put up much of a fight. It felt like dried leaves.

When his anger had subsided, he fell into a restless sleep. He slept most of the day, with the bits of dried sack scattered around him. He wanted to catch the plague and go where Gili was. But when he woke in the night, he was still there, unharmed by the terrible disease.

When he went outside into the pre-dawn light, he could hear some young caterpillars laughing and playing. He thought, "They remind me of the young scorpions from my own kingdom, full of energy and never sleeping." Daev knew that he did not belong there anymore, so he decided to make the journey back home.

Head down, he dragged his tail behind him and sadly walked toward the gates.

As he approached the caterpillars, a very young one came up to him and said, "Our queen loved you very much and spoke of you often. But you know she's not dead, don't you?"

Daev looked at the young caterpillar in amazement. "What do you mean?"

The young caterpillar explained that he had lost his grandfather to the plague, and had stayed up all day and night watching the lime green sack. When it eventually turned brown and dried up—lo and behold—a beautiful butterfly had emerged! He knew it was his grandfather because the butterfly had similar stripes.

The young caterpillar continued, "He flew and landed on top of me, and I could sense it was my grandfather. He had taken a different form, that's all. There are others who have seen this, but everyone thinks we're crazy and making it up."

The other little caterpillars were laughing at him. "Daev, don't listen to him; he's been drinking too much nectar," they said.

The little caterpillar insisted it was true. "Some have seen it but others haven't, and people don't believe in things they don't see. But I saw it happen!"

Daev smiled. "I think I understand. I can't see at all, but I do have other senses that are keener than yours." Daev thanked the little caterpillar for sharing his story with him, but he remained so sad that he could only focus on his loss. He could not stay with the caterpillars without his beloved Gili, so he set out for home and to his parents.

CHAPTER 17
A Scorpion and a Butterfly

"What the caterpillar calls the end of the world, the master calls a butterfly."
—Richard Bach

Daev walked day and night. His journey was hard, and he was surprised that the owls did not attack him and that other danger seemed to avoid him too. Perhaps he appeared sick, or maybe he was somehow protected from the unknown.

Daev did not realize that Gili had indeed turned into the most beautiful Queen butterfly. In fact, she had watched Daev return to her kingdom and had felt terribly sad when he began to grieve. She now fluttered all around him, but Daev was too upset to even sense her presence. His head hung down, and because she was in a different form and vibrated at a slightly different rate than she had before, he couldn't feel that she was above him. She was visible, but not to Daev. The young caterpillars must have been more open to seeing butterflies because they were pure and had open minds. The older caterpillars were much too busy eating milkweeds all day and resting to even bother to look up.

Gili followed Daev on his journey back home. When the owls tried to eat him, she flew in between them causing a distraction, and when large desert mice came, she landed on their backs, flapping her wings. Daev didn't notice.

He would not have cared if he had been eaten. He was so sad, and his loss of hope made Gili very sad. Up in her new world, she

saw everything from a different perspective. There was so much of
life to explore and learn about. There were trees of all types, large
animals, small animals, lakes, and rivers. She learned of new things
like people and strange metal boxes with wheels. There were birds
up there, too, soaring high in the sky as if to boast that they had a
better view than she did. She could feel the wind under her wings
and could tell if there was a storm coming, and the flowers were so
beautiful when she looked down inside them.

"Oh, Daev," she pleaded, "there is so much of life to explore."
But whatever she said, and however much she flapped around him,

he remained unaware of her. Although she could see him, he could no longer hear her. She was on a higher plane now.

When Daev returned home, everyone in the kingdom felt his grief. Daev went straight to his room, where he stayed for weeks. His mother tried her best to speak to him, but he did not respond. He did manage to tell her that Gili had caught the plague and disappeared, but that was all he said. Even Daev's father could feel his son's pain.

Gili was trying her best to get into the crevice that led to Daev's room, but it was much too small. She spent most of the day eating milkweeds—still her favorite food—and in the evening she slept outside his cave, above his room, hoping to catch his attention.

Daev's mother eventually persuaded him to venture out and get some food, which Daev reluctantly did. He mostly ate at night and Gili tried to attract his attention, but Daev did not even feel her presence.

Then one day, Daev ventured out in the sunlight, and Gili could tell that he was remembering how they had spent their days together. Daev put a large leaf on his back and walked around. He walked to the milkweed bushes and stopped near a rock. Tears dropped from above his mouth, and Gili could not keep from crying herself. She landed next to him and saw the hairs on his body responding to her presence. Finally! She had got through to him! He became tense as he looked around and prepared his tail to strike. Daev didn't know what was next to him, but he sensed something. Then he relaxed.

At last he smiled. "Gili, is that you? Are you a butterfly like the young caterpillar said?"

"Yes, Daev, it's me!" Gili cried in delight. But she realized that he could not hear her. Her voice was too soft, and she vibrated at a different frequency. If only Daev had eyes! Then he would see her! She fluttered all around him, even landing on his back. Daev felt her presence and smiled. Somehow he knew that Gili would always be close by, even though he couldn't hear her anymore.

Gili stayed with Daev, protecting him throughout his life, and at times she knew he felt her presence. Sometimes she joined her parents, who were also butterflies. Like them, she had work to do as a Queen butterfly. Life was wonderful and she had learned so much as a caterpillar. She flew with joy when Daev ventured out and learned as much as he could too.

"We will forever be connected," Gili thought and laughed. "Such a strange pair indeed—a scorpion and a butterfly. . . ."

Glossary

Arachnida   (ə-răk′nĭda)

    A class of insects that includes spiders, scorpions, mites, and ticks

Batesian mimicry   (bāt′sē-ən mím-ik-ree)

    When an animal or insect copies the coloring of another animal or insect for protection from predators

camouflage   (kăm′ə-fläj′)

    An animal or insect's natural coloring or form that enables it to blend with its surroundings

chelicerae   (kĭ-lĭs′ər-ə)

    A pair of appendages (like teeth) in the front of the mouth in arachnids; pincer-like claws

chrysalis   (krĭs′ə-lĭs)

    The hard outer case or pupa that encases the caterpillar before it turns into a butterfly

cocoon   (kə-kōōn′)

    A silky case spun by larvae of insects for protection

delicacy   (dĕl′ĭ-kə-sē)
   A choice or expensive food

epidermis   (ĕp′ĭ-dûr′mĭs)
   The outer layer of skin or cells covering the true skin

fluoresce   (flŏŏ-rĕs′)
   Shine or glow brightly

genera   (jĕn′ər-ə)
   A group of insects or organisms having similar character-
   istics

glycoside   (glī′-kə-sīd′)
   A compound formed by simple sugar and another compound; poison from plants

impermeable   (ĭm-pûr′mē-ə-bəl)
   Not allowing fluid to pass through

instinctive   (ĭn-stĭngk′tĭv)
   Doing something automatically or naturally

larva   (lär′və)
   An immature form of an insect; the stage between egg and
   pupa

metamorphosis   (mĕt′ə-môr′fə-sĭs)
>The process of change from an immature form to an adult form in two or more stages; a change of the form or nature of an insect into a completely different one by natural means (ex. caterpillar into a butterfly)

mimic   (mĭm′ĭk)
>To resemble or imitate another insect or animal to deter predators or for camouflage

myth   (mĭth)
>Widely held false belief or idea

nectar   (nĕk′tər)
>A sugary fluid secreted by plants, especially within flowers

nocturnal   (nŏk-tûr′nəl)
>Active at night

ominous   (ŏm′ə-nəs)
>The impression something bad or unpleasant is going to happen

pigmentation   (pĭg′mən-tā′shən)
>The natural coloring of an insect, plant tissue, or animal

pincer   (pĭn′sər)
> A front claw of a scorpion, lobster, or crab

plague   (plāg)
> A contagious disease that spreads rapidly and kills many

predator   (prĕd′ə-tər)
> An animal or insect that preys or hunts for food; its food is usually smaller animals and insects

proboscis   (prō-bós′ĭs)
> A long sucking mouthpart that is Tube-like and flexible in insects

pupa   (pyōō′pə)
> An insect in its "inactive" immature form between larva and adult; a chrysalis

radiation   (rā′dē-ā′shən)
> A process in which energy is emitted as particles or waves; energy transmitted in the way of heat light, electricity, etc.

troglobite   (trŏg′lə-bīt)
> An insect or animal that lives mainly in the dark part of a cave

ultraviolet   (ŭl′trə-vī′ə-lĕt)
    Found in sunlight; it can cause chemical reactions that can
    allow many substances to glow or fluoresce

venom   (vĕn′əm)
    Poisonous fluid secreted by animals such as snakes and
    scorpions usually injected into prey by biting or stinging

Pronunciations

Dana Gilippus   (Dan-us Gil-ipp-us)

Superstitioniidae   (sōō′pər-stĭsh′ən-i-day)